THE CITY:

A Story in 140 Characters

Hugh J. O'Donnell

001: Dawn

Dawn loomed over The City. She stood and watched the rising sun filter through block after block from her vantage on the roof of Midas Corp. Tower. She had climbed up without light, making the perilous trip by memory and relying on a FAQ when the going got tough. There wasn't anything up here, but it was the best view short of buying your own plane. And who had the credits to waste on something like that? This was her city, and she was its vagabond master. It was a new day, and below her adventure was waiting. She jumped.

002: Augustus

Augustus watched the sunrise from the floor-to-ceiling window of the 97th floor boardroom. They had worked through the night, but the contract was finished. Everyone but he and the client had gone home. He was the fifth-richest man in the world, and this sale would multiply his fortune. But could he really give up his control of Midas Corp? Could he leave The City behind? A rainbow parachute descended past him. A punky girl in black leather dangled from it. She met his eye and gave him the finger. He crossed back to the table and signed.

003: Gina

Gina watched the jumper on the exterior cameras. Her chute was a cheap model, without any stabilizers. You could get one of those for the credits you'd find lying in the street. The kid was a Daytripper, not a Citizen like her. And she didn't know how strong the crosswinds blew up here. They buzzed for her in the conference room. They must have finally finished. She wished the kid happy landings, and went in. The signed contract lay on the table. The mysterious gentleman looked happy, but her boss just looked tired. She took it, and left the room.

004: Bob

Bob knew every turn and corner in The City. He could get from The Heights to The Bay inside of ten minutes, in any weather, at any time of day. He'd been a driver for Midas Corp. for five years, and he'd been Augustus Sizemore's chauffeur for two. Before that, he'd been a Daytripping Gearhead. Once he was the king of the underground street racing circuit. But everybody has to grow up and get a real job sometime. The doors opened and two men got in. One was his boss, the other, he did not know. Bob started the engine.

005: Laura

Laura was the owner of a very exclusive night club. She'd had a long, lucrative night, but it was morning now. The dance floor was empty, the chairs had been placed on the tables, and the the rest of the staff had gone home. She should be home, too. But you can get anything at any time in The City. Especially if you're Augustus Sizemore. So she opened up and brought them a bottle of champagne. She poured herself for the CEO and his guest. She marveled at how prettily it sparkled in the new day's sunlight. They clinked glasses.

006: The Buyer

Augustus watched the other man over his glass. He was still smiling that damned Guy Fawkes grin. He'd never seen it falter, no matter how hard he negotiated. And he was just as good. A world champion poker player. But now the game was over. "So now that you've got my stake, what will you do with it?"

He set down his glass. "My backers think like you do. The City is an efficient way of concentrating capital. But I see it as so much more than that. There is so much potential here. I'm going to do wonderful things."

007: Emily

The City was the center of the world, and Emily sat on the throne. At least, that is how she considered her desk at Midas Bank. The City, and by extension Midas, had become the world's clearing house. Every day, Billions of Dollars, Euros, Yen, Yuan, Pounds, and every other trading currency flowed through her gates, were converted to credits, passed through a few more hands, and left again. She logged the transactions and sped the bundles on their way. She didn't know much about international finance law, but that wasn't her department. She was certain everything was completely legal.

008: Norm

Twenty floors below, the Personal Banking Center was opening its doors. People preferred to do their banking in The City. Midas was very proud of the fact that they had never been robbed since they were open. Or so City Records would have you believe.

There's a first time for everything, Norm thought, adjusting his glasses and hat using a chromed pillar. He waited around the lobby for a cubicle drone, and made a careful catalog of entrances, exits, cameras, and visible security measures. It could be done. He tried not to smirk during the mortgage consultation. It wasn't easy.

009: Sandra

The City's lifeblood was the Metro. From the Underground to the L-Trains. Elites might be able to afford cars and drivers, but Citizens and and Daytrippers alike had to ride mass transit. They ran from every corner of The City. Sandra took one from her shoebox apartment to her Midas Corp Office every day. Until they unjustly fired her. But what could she do? Midas was a power unto themselves here. She was despondent. Until he appeared. He gave her the key and told her how to fight back. His smile was so understanding. Today, the trains would stop.

010: Frank

Frank was a train driver for The City. It was a good job, even if it didn't pay well. It beat slinging burgers. It beat just about any job he could get Outside. And Frank's options were very limited.

The crash had been an accident. But after getting his 'time to think,' he understood that accidents weren't just products of random chance, but bad decisions. One bad decision had caused so much suffering. At least in The City, he could still drive a train. He eased her into Commercial Station.

The woman stepped from the platform just ahead of him.

011: Xue

Xue was feeding the ducks when she got Dawn's message. She liked ducks. They didn't build, didn't destroy, didn't do anything but swim and eat bread crumbs. Feeding the ducks was her favorite thing to do in the City. It was a retreat, a meditation from the pressure and demands of school and family. It was not that she was ungrateful. Her future was being formed like a diamond by that pressure. But too much and she would collapse instead. She listened to it twice, gave up and ran the translation.

"Please come pick me up? I'm kind of stuck."

012: Stepan

Stepan watched the girl from his monitoring station at Door 37 of Midas Corp Headquarters. He could have helped her, but that would have meant leaving his post, and he would surely catch hell for it later. She was a Daytripper, and thus below Midas' notice. She was unsightly, but causing no disturbance. Orders hadn't come down to remove her, so he was content to leave her be.

Instead, he monitored his investments on a secure channel. He heard from Gina that The Man Himself had sold his shares. The sale was still secret, but what shockwaves would it release?

013: Cleopatra

Cleopatra watched the commotion in the train station with interest. She liked these kinds of gatherings. All the people, the noise, the chaos. This was why she was in The City. Citizens and Daytrippers ignored her, and she preferred it that way. All the better to watch them in their rushing patterns. The City was a different beast to her, and she knew all its hidden passages. Maybe that is why only Cleopatra noticed the man with the smile frozen on his lips. Then he turned and quite impossibly, vanished. The little calico cat did not understand, but only watched.

014: Ingmar

Dawn hadn't been very specific, but it sounded like they would need a car, at the very least. The only friend Xue knew in The City that had one was Ingmar, but he and Dawn did not get along. Great. She booted her phone's translator and connected.

"Hi, it's Xue. I need you to do me a favor…"

Traffic was glacial throughout The City. It took them two hours to reach the financial district. The sight of Dawn dangling helplessly from a gargoyle was worth it though. Ingmar laughed so hard he barely recorded her annoyed frown without camera shake.

015: Julia

Julia had been a cop in The City for over five years. Some of her friends had chided her for taking such a safe assignment, but she didn't care. The City had rules just like anyplace else, and of course special care had to be applied in enforcing them. But this was nothing she'd trained for. She called dispatch.

"Marcy, this is Julia out in Commerce Station.. I've got one hell of a case here."

"What's up?"

"Jane Doe jumped at a moving train as it was entering the platform."

"That shouldn't happen."

"That's not even it. There's a body."

016: Govad

From his office on the 48th floor, Govad read the reports. They were not good news. He was looking at a situation so outlandish, so downright impossible, that he didn't even have the barest bones of a response for it. To make matters worse, he could not get in touch with superiors for instructions. It was like the entire Board of Directors took a vacation at once. Things like this didn't happen at Midas Corp. But he was Director of Mass Transit, and this was what they paid him to do. He called up the messaging system and began typing.

017: Iva

Iva jogged through Sizemore's Grove, the upscale, suburban neighborhood where well-off citizens started their day. She was a Daytripper herself, but she liked the route. The occasional presence of guards, dogs, and even once a security drone which hovered behind her for half a mile and took pot-shots at her, made training more invigorating. Her Messenger flashed and squawked before turning on in automatic mode. It was a public safety message.

"Attentional all City Residents. Mass Transit will be shut down for routine maintenance until further notice. Thank you for your patience." Iva smirked. Commuters. She kept running.

018: Abner

Abner arrived late to work. Even in The City, the trains wouldn't run on time. There was still so much human error, still so few backup systems. And it had to be during rush hour. Of course in The City, it was always rush hour someplace. But naturally it was during his commute on the day of his evaluation. He braced for a siren as he badged in. He was going to climb up to the 48th floor and kick someone's teeth in. He froze in the lobby. "Sizemore Sells Shares to International Investors" was plastered on every monitor. Awesome.

019: Melinda

Melinda looked into the camera like it was the face of every one of her hundred-million viewers.

"Once again, our top story this morning: Augustus Sizemore, CEO and Majority Stockholder of Midas Corp has reportedly sold his shares and is stepping down from his role as Chairperson. A statement released this morning did not name the purchasing party, and the Company itself has yet to make a statement. Midas Corp is the operator of 'The City,' a realistic virtual environment which employs hundreds of thousands of people and has millions of users. Markets are reacting sharply to the announcement."

020: Floyd

The Meals-On-Wheels truck arrived at the house on time for breakfast. Floyd readied the tray and rang the bell. Sandra was one of his favorite clients. She'd seen a lot of hardships in her life, and a bad car accident had left her housebound. She fought on though. She'd taken a job with Midas, and was so proud of the complicated rig of goggles and gear that let her lead a Normal Life in The City. When nobody answered, he peeked in a window. He saw her body sprawled On her office floor, and immediately called emergency services.

021: Zophia

Zophia set her spiders to work. Thanks to the anonymous email she received that morning, many were already prepared. They made their webs in every stock market across the world. And as the world spun and each woke up to the news that The City was changing hands, her programs fed on the panic. As the girl watched her bank accounts fatten, she almost felt bad for Sizemore, and the foolish little brokers who were watching their charges' retirements slip through their fingers. Because they weren't prepared. Later, she would have to back trace the message. For now, she fed.

022: Norbert

Melinda turned to Camera 2.

"And now, I'd like to turn to International Finance expert Norbert Finkelmeyer. Good Morning."

"Good morning Melinda."

"What does this Midas deal mean?"

"It is effectively the sale of The City itself, because Midas Corp built and maintains it."

"Why is that important?"

"Due to the hyper-realistic nature of The City, and the lax tax laws on the island nation where its servers are kept, Midas is the leading Financial Services firm in the world. Trillions of dollars move through the city every second."

"What effect will this sale have?"

"We don't know yet."

023: Dorothy

Dorothy was an assassin of improbable accidents. She made her living off a loophole in The City's laws.

The City was a simulation, but it behaved as though it were a real place. An avatar was fragile; subject to gravity, fire, and trauma. A user only had one Avatar to lose. Dying in The City could be more inconvenient and financially devastating than anywhere on Earth. There were no guns in The City, but Dorothy had her methods. She specialized in Houses, but had other tricks and devices.

On the day Midas was sold, her email account crashed from overuse.

024: Hiro

They gathered in Midas Park. Stretching the whole middle of The City, the green space was a patchwork of famous public spaces from a hundred terrestrial cities, and others so fanciful they could only have been designed there.

Hiro waited in front of Osaka Castle. There, the cherry blossoms always fell, and it had an excellent view of The Sphinx and Old Faithful. Plus, he could see the building-sized screens covering the announcement. A milling crowd of Daytrippers and uncertain Citizens were already gathered beneath them. It was several hours before Dawn and the others arrived, looking completely frazzled.

025: Marcy

Lieutenant Marcy, along with Commissioner Jenkins and a delegation of IT and QA people, met Julia and the corpse in the City Morgue. As far as she knew, it was the first time it had ever been used. After pleasantries, one of them played coroner and conducted an examination. Aside from its already missing head, the corpse remained intact.

"Well, it's certainly malicious code," he said.

"Can you ID her?" Marcy asked.

"No, her credentials have been scrambled. This is nasty stuff."

"Can we boot the user?" Jenkins asked.

"The eject code isn't responding."

And then the corpse sat upright.

026: Nick

After the scene was cleared, Frank had to meet with his manager, Nick. He was badly shaken, and in no mood to deal with the weaselly paper-pusher.

"How the hell could you screw up like this, Frank?" The little toad asked.

"She shouldn't have been able to do that. It's against the rules…"

"But you hit her anyway, just like you hit that kid…" Frank snapped. He stoop up and decked him. His avatar registered the hit and collapsed. Nick didn't feel it, though. Frank was too angry to care.

"That's the last straw, dumbass," Nick huffed. "You're Gone!"

027: Renee

The shoebox apartment wasn't much to look at. It didn't even have a window. It was just a single light bulb, a card table, and a phone. The only thing she had to look at was Norm pacing and mumbling to himself three feet away. She knew enough about virtual architecture to know that this room could be any size, filled with whatever they could imagine. But they needed to remain anonymous and inconspicuous. Breaking The City's rules would bring notice. The phone rang and she answered.

"I understand. The meeting's tonight. You know where." She hung up. "Frank's in."

028: MacBeth

MacBeth the Cat sunned himself on an outer wall of Osaka Castle. He enjoyed the spot because it was always warm and sunny during the day, and there were many small birds and squirrels to chase. Below him, a crowd of humans, teenagers, he noted, was gathering. Lazily, he cataloged and recorded their identities and conversation. He wasn't listening, but the recording went on automatically. A pair of additional humans climbed the steps and joined the group. A girl, identified as Nora O'Reilly, location: Donegal, Ireland, reached up a hand to pet him. He hissed, and bounded into the grass.

029: Nora

Nora frowned after the cat and sat down on the bench next to Hiro. She furiously typed into her messenger. Between the six of them, they spoke ten languages, but there wasn't one they all shared fluently. So they typed, even sitting on the same bench.

Paulo and I had an awful time getting here. The trains are all shut down. Nora wrote.

A woman got hit by one. Hiro replied.

Impossible.

Is it? Dawn typed. *Or is it just so unlikely that it never happened before? The Man sold out and the trains stop. No such thing as coincidence.*

030: Paulo

Paulo nodded to the American punk girl.

Do you think the one has to do with the other? Is Midas screwing with the trains to manipulate the market?

Xue shook her head.

Too expensive. Midas owns too much of The City to wreck its productivity.

Maybe a rival? Ingmar asked.

The timing's too close. The trains stopped running before the sale was announced.

I got a peek at the meeting. The new CEO's avatar looked weird.

Weird how?

I don't know. Out of sync. Kind of creepy.

I'll look into it, offered Paulo. He was always trying to impress Dawn.

031: Janelle

In the decorative morgue, the former avatar of Sandra sat upright and looked around. At least, it gave the impression that it was looking around. Half of its head was missing. Janelle stepped forward.

"Contact with the user must have been reestablished," she said. "Hello, I'm Janelle Smith, with Midas Quality Control. We'd like to talk with out about your user experience." The living corpse turned to look at her, and screamed in a robotic voice.

"Change is coming to The City! Death is coming to The City! Destruction is coming to The City!" It collapsed back onto the gurney.

032: Maurice

City Police Commissioner Maurice Jenkins was the first to press close to the body when it began to whisper.

"The Hills, The Bay, The Valley, The tower. The Bells! The bells are ringing. The clarion call is sounding and He is coming to draw the threads together. He'll climb Jacob's ladder and descend from fire as the phoenix. The City will know its master, and He will be the god of this place. The bells..." The corpse went still.

"Some hacker messing with us," Marcy said.

Maurice frowned. "I'd like to speak with the hacker that did this. Let's go."

033: Meghan

A long line of police cars, their sirens blaring, raced out of Headquarters. They were followed by a smaller fleet of unmarked, black vehicles. They traveled at all possible speed to Midas Corporation Tower, at the heart of The City. It was not so far from Police Headquarters, but traffic was backed up due to the transit shutdown. Meghan had the pleasure of listening to the Commissioner swear the entire way.

"Bells, what the fuck does that mean?" Back at headquarters, an entire squad was puzzling over the prophetic riddle.

They stopped short. Midas Plaza was blocked off by Security.

034: Ray

Ray had the fortunate duty of being the guard that met City Police when they showed up en masse. Just what he needed, the damn VR cops. As far as he was concerned they were set dressing, like everything else in The City. They were paper tigers.

Midas Security, they were the real thing, with their Boot Guns and the writ of Midas's board to do anything they needed to protect the real owners of The City. Public safety? What a joke. Meghan rolled down the window of her cruiser.

"You can't come in," he said. "There's a board meeting."

035: Victoria

At the other end of the compound, Victoria watched without interest as her driver negotiated the limousine through the checkpoint. Heightened security bothered her. The first change was not a reassuring one. And for a virtual bank of all things. It would be ludicrous if the threats they faced weren't so serious. Getting killed in the real world was risky, but getting assassinated in The City, losing her access, possibly even being hacked, that was what kept her up at night. And the changeover would be a prime opportunity for an attack. Sizemore's replacement had better be good, she thought.

036: Glenn

In Midas Corp's opulent 97th floor board room, Glenn went from chair to chair, preparing the board's regalia. There was a manila folder, complete with simulated documents, as well as a tablet detailing the sale between Sizemore and the new owner. A legal pad, a selection of pens and pencils, even a cup of coffee. It was all strictly symbolic. The board would bring their own implements slaved to record and message. But The City's kabuki of the physical world was of the upmost importance, and interns had to play their part. The Smiling Man nodded, and Glenn exited discreetly.

037: Kat

Kat was the first to arrive. She passed the intern going out. Kat gave him a friendly smile, because no one was around. She was the youngest shareholder, but she'd be damned if she was going to let anyone push her around because she was an heiress, or because the three percent of stock she owned was barely enough to qualify for a seat at the head table, rather than the bigger meeting later in the week. She was a tiger, and she could afford to be patient. She could afford to be kind, as long as nobody was looking.

038: Trey

Trey took his rightful seat at the head of the table. A few of the others had already arrived, mostly tech hotshots and other youngsters. Sizemore was not among them. Trey had been one of the principal investors in Midas, and he had invested millions in the company, but he never spent a second longer than he had to in The City. He hated computers, but he knew a good pitch when he heard it, and Sizemore had delivered. That made his absence now all the more galling.

"The Coward didn't even show up to his own resignation," he grumbled.

039: Linda

Linda patted Trey's arm in what she hoped looked like a grandmotherly way. Not that she'd ever touch him in real life, but the gesture was for the cameras each of them had secreted about their persons. Her PR people would leak it later. Linda considered herself the Grand Dame of the twelve member board, and she had chosen to play this acquisition soft, for now.

"I'm sure dear Augustus has a good reason for his absence, and our new associates have a good reason for remaining anonymous, for now." The Smiling Man said nothing. The board found their seats.

040: Gene

Gene was the last member of the board to arrive. The retired entertainer was used to making people wait for him, so he was not particularly bothered by the ten pairs of glaring eyes staring daggers at him. He was even less interested in the man in the cheap avatar up front, the mysterious bag man for whomever had bought Sizemore out. Gene had headlined The City's first live concert, a proof of concept that elevated it from nerd hangout to international hot spot. Let them stare and fight each other for scraps. His seat on the board was assured.

041: Ilyana

Ilyana took careful notes as the man began his presentation. The first five minutes were all bland platitudes, as cheap and hollow as his avatar. He introduced himself as Alan Babbage, a pseudonym so facile it was insulting. He continued to deflect the question of who his backers were, which made it all but certain that the deal was illegal. And while The City had risen to prominence by being a digital haven more secure than a chain of Cayman Islands stacked on top of Dubai, there would come a tipping point. And Ilyana would be ready when it did.

042: Sam

Sam was an oil baron. His daddy had been an oil baron. His son, if he didn't bankrupt the company or buy a baseball team or some damn thing, would be one too. Sam knew there was a lot going on in this room. It wasn't a real space, but with his gloves and goggles on, it might as well have been. Everything else was fake, too. The smiles, the platitudes. The board was a nest of vipers, but this new guy, Babbage, he was different. His frozen face just as fraudulent, but he wore it openly. Sam liked that.

043: Dani

Dani watched the rest of the board, waiting for the resentment to break the surface. She wondered who would crack first. Would it be Victoria, Sizemore's able second in command? How much did she know about this deal? Or would it be Raine, the angel investor who kept Midas afloat when it was the whipping boy of a phalanx of international justice probes? Or would it be Trey and Linda, the venture capitalists that got The City off the ground without knowing what it was? It turned out to Roberto, the Brazilian social media wunderkind, who threw the first punch.

044: Roberto

For Roberto, the stock sale was the final insult. He had never been a loyal soldier to Midas Corp. Their takeover of his company had been all but openly hostile, but the price had been too good to pass up, and The City needed his translation algorithms and messaging capability to become what it was today. Sizemore had never trusted him, and he admitted it was probably with good reason. But to sell his shares without consulting the board, Roberto included, was unconscionable. Roberto banged his fist on the table. "I demand an explanation," he shouted to the grinning idiot.

045: Raine

"An explanation? Of course." Babbage practically oozed unctuous charm. Raine considered the confrontation with interest. The whole board did, but they weren't going to get involved. There was a time to get your hands dirty, and a time to keep them clean. Most of them knew which was which. "I believe you'll find a document in your folders which explains the situation quite clearly." Roberto ripped out the paper in question and held it up.

"This doesn't tell me a goddam thing!" Holding the paper, Roberto's avatar suddenly glitched and froze in place. Babbage smile seemed to widen.

"Let's begin."

046: Tyrone

Downstairs, the situation was getting tense between City Police and the Midas Private Security. Commissioner Jenkins had nearly fought his way inside, and all available security converged to stop them from entering.

The problem was, the cops were unbootable and unbannable, which made Tyrone and the other guards' weapons useless. But if the cops' were, so were the security guards'. They were at an impasse. Some twit, a suit low enough on the ladder to get thrown to the wolves, identified as Abner Lanning, appealed for calm as the meeting continued in the executive boardroom. He was bootable.

Tyrone fired.

047: Emma

Something was happening in the lobby. Emma tried to check her feeds, something she added for herself when she built the system. She couldn't pull them. Babbage glared straight at her. He knew! How could he know? And what had he done to Roberto?

"You've hacked The City," she said. "I didn't think it was possible." The rest of the board stared in horror.

"Hacking is such an inelegant word for what I've done. I've remade The City in my own image. I needed just Sizemore's access to finish."

"What are you going to do," she asked. "Crown yourself king?"

048: Jake

On the other side of the city, Jake, a data entry clerk for one of Midas's competitors, took his fifteen minute break. He wasn't allowed to log out, which made getting up to use the bathroom a challenge, but at least he could check his email. There was a message from Midasoft announcing a new patch. The source was verified, but the content just had a vague message about performance and stability upgrades. He wasn't supposed to download during work hours, but he was on break, so Damn The Man. He skimmed through the EULA and clicked the 'install' button.

049: Loraine

Loraine watched the boardroom from her monitor. Something funny was going on. It wasn't her job as security guard to meddle, but Mr. Constantino hadn't moved for two solid minutes. She was sure the new CEO had done something to his avatar somehow. She pinged the boardroom, but nobody picked up.

"King?" Babbage laughed, pacing the room. "I want nothing so small. Sizemore had so much access, so much control that he never utilized. Myself? I will be a god!" CEO or not, Loraine had to get the board out. She ran into the hall. The boardroom door was gone.

050:
Rosencrantz

Rosencrantz the cat was hunting his digital prey, mostly interesting shadows and blowing leaves, as there were few mice or insects to catch in The City. He began to notice the humans acting strangely. They stood very still, often in the middle of the street, an action he barely understood to mean their attention was elsewhere. Then, they began to change. They slumped over or growled, and moved in unnatural ways or behaved oddly.

Rosencrantz didn't understand what a 'zombie' was, but as panic erupted throughout The City, he slunk back into the shadows. Shakespeare would know what to do.

051: Cynthia

Boot guns worked on a simple principle. Normally, a person could only exit or enter The City from a 'house' where they had access. Some allowances are made for access interruptions, but improper logouts were deemed criminal offenses. This reinforced the illusion and also prevented 'Dropout Syndrome.' DS was a neurological condition discovered in Beta when users exited The City too quickly. Midas paid millions to cover up the damage and created housing to fix the problem.

They also made Boot Guns to forcibly remove troublemakers.

Which was why Cynthia was surprised when her gun did nothing against the zombies.

052: Mario

Mario glared at Loraine. CPD was storming the damn tower, and here she was raving about magic and disappearing doors. He did not have time to deal with her stupidity today. He sighed.

"You can't change the physical reality of The City. It's one of The Rules."

"Rules set by Sizemore. What if this guy got past Sizemore to get to the board?" Mario shook his head.

"Well, I have to report the riot anyway. Let's go. Lopez, you come with us." The door was perfectly visible when the three of them got there.

"But it was gone!"

Mario knocked.

053: Tina

Tina shot Lorraine a smug look as Mario knocked on the towering mahogany doors. She'd been after Loraine's spot on the Executive Security Team, and now it was practically her's! Unless the cops downstairs did something stupid like try and occupy the building or invoke their emergency powers. A Coup would ruin everything.

Mario opened the door and went in.

"I'm sorry to disturb you, ladies and gentlemen, but we have a security situation, and we have to ask you to evacuate." Twelve smiling faces turned at once to look at them.

"I'm just about done here anyway," Babbage said.

054: Warren

In a quieter part of The City, Warren knocked on the door of a rundown apartment. Midas could have made every one a luxury penthouse, but where was the money in that? Renee cracked the door and let him in. Six people were crammed around a card table. It wasn't a big crew, but it was large enough for complications. He didn't know most of them.

"Do you have them?" Norm asked from his folding chair. Warren pulled out a bag and upended it on the faux leather surface.

"Seven boot guns," he said. "Stripped and ready for avatar bonding."

055: Mina

Mina looked down at the guns and back up at the man with the bag. Someone, the train driver, whistled. She frowned. This didn't smell right. "How did you get so many clean guns?" She asked.

"CPD headquarters has been going nuts all day. It was easy to sneak down to the supply terminal, fake my boss's access, and grab them. We'll hit the bank and be gone before anyone knows they were fabricated."

"But how will we bond with them?" Ingmar, the youngest of the group, asked. "We don't have clearance for that."

"Leave that to me," Renee said.

056: Nigel

"Welcome back to News Focus, I'm your host Nigel Smyth. Today's topic is "The City: virtual paradise, or secret health risk?" With me today is Boot Syndrome expert Dr. Ophira Nottingham, noted futurist Jonathan Isaacs, and BBC Tech Corespondent Douglas Pine. Plus, a special report from Starla Roberts in America. Thank you all for being here." Nigel turned to the table of panelists. He had been against the topic. He could barely use his laptop, and now he had to sit through four nerds debating effects of eye strain. He smiled warmly for the camera. "Doctor, let's start with you…"

057: Ophira

Ophira sat back in her chair and waited. She tried not to look contemptuous as the host worked his way towards an intelligent question. He didn't quite make it.

"Doctor, what is Boot Syndrome?"

"Virtual Reality Displacement Disorder, or 'Boot Syndrome' is a medical condition caused by suddenly shifting from a high-resolution virtual environment, such as The City, back to the real world."

"Is it dangerous?" Ophira needed to have a serious talk with her booking agent.

"It can have a wide range of effects, from simple headaches to lasting neurological trauma, and even death, in a few cases."

058: Jonathan

Jonathan scoffed. "A few cases, Doctor? The City has a user base of over a billion people! It has been running for over five years, and since the beginning, proper use of Logout Housing has effectively proven that the technology running The City is safe and reliable. There are even safeguards for interrupted connections and power outages with the latest updates. The City is perfectly safe!" He slammed his fist on the table for emphasis. He was a paltry stockholder in Midas Corp, but even his few shares had made him a rich man. He planned on staying that way.

059: Starla

"If I may," said the American woman, live on feed from Virginia.

"Yes, Ms. Roberts, Go ahead."

"I'm at the home of Sandra Davis, a City user who was discovered dead early this morning. Investigations are still ongoing. CPD and Midas Corp have not commented, but reports indicate she was struck by a commuter train in The City itself. Ms. Davis was already in frail health after a car accident last year."

"That is quite frankly impossible," Jonathan cut her off.

"And yet," Nigel responded, "Thousands of users have uploaded recordings of the incident." Isaacs grimaced, but had no response.

060: Douglas

Nigel turned to the last member of the panel. "Let's bring in our Tech Corespondent on this point. Douglas, could a virtual train kill a living person?" Douglas pushed the glasses up on his nose.

"Well, 'deaths' in The City are often traumatic. This seems to be an unprecedented event. Train lines were completely shut down this morning. As for how it happened, some users are reporting malware disguised as an update causing issues. She may have downloaded a virus." Nigel didn't know what any of that meant, and neither did his audience, but they'd be sure to stay tuned.

061: Georgia

In the lobby of Midas Corporate Tower, the tide was turning in the Police's favor. Sgt. Georgia Ramirez, formerly NYPD, found it to be the strangest assault she'd ever been a part of. Neither side could really harm the other, and the boot guns were out of play. The cops has their cuffs, which immobilized a target, but were difficult to use. Midas Security had stunners, which were easier to use, but wore off quickly. In the end, it came down to numbers. Moving in tight circles, Georgia and the other officers surrounded the Midas guards, tackled, and cuffed them.

062: Miles

Miles closed the cuff on the last lobby guard and gave the commissioner a thumbs up. The cops frisked their prisoners and relieved them of any errant stunners still in their inventories. Commissioner Jenkins set up his command post and started giving out orders.

"We go floor by floor. We don't know what we're looking for, so report anything suspicious. Cuff any Security you find. Anybody else causes trouble, give 'em the boot." Miles formed up with his squad, eager for more excitement.

Several floors below, Babbage's limousine slid out of the parking garage and into an unmarked service tunnel.

063: Deborah

Deborah's team got the short straw. They had to clear the top-floor offices. She took point, stunner in one hand, boot gun in the other. The palatial Executive Suite of Midas Holdings was deserted. All they found were empty rooms. The digital marble echoed with their simulated footfalls. Deborah shivered, forgetting she was in an Arizona office park.

She went to a filing cabinet and opened it. It was completely empty. It should have held Midas's financial data, but there was nothing to link to. Deborah stared into a void.

The rest of the squad continued into the office.

064:Kumar

Two miles away, Sizemore's former limousine led half a dozen CPD patrol cars on a chase though the downtown corridor. They should've been able to easily corner the black stretch behemoth. Somehow, it kept ahead of them; weaving through impossible gaps in the mid-day traffic and drifting around corners.

"Who's driving that thing?" Officer Kumar Sodhi punched his steering wheel.

"I heard it was Bob Tolstoy," his partner replied.

"The street racer? When did he turn legit?"

"A few years back. Everybody's got to eat." As they watched, siren blaring uselessly, the limo glided onto the highway and disappeared.

065: Lucinda

Lucinda and the rest of her squad burst into the palatial office of Midas's CEO's office expecting a siege. But it was as empty as the rest of the floor. Nothing remained. No papers, no terminals, just a wide expanse of simulated mahogany, and the bomb.

It looked like something out of a cartoon. Cherry-red sticks of TNT were connected by a rainbow of curly wires to a softly ticking clock.

Roger reached out to touch it, and she slapped his hand before thumbing her com.

"We need an evac of the building. There's a bomb on Sizemore's desk."

066: Thom

Thom stared down at the desk in consternation. He was the Chief Bomb Disposal technician for the CPD. Of course, up until now the title had been a joke. Explosives, along with most other kinds of weapons, not only didn't exist in The City, but couldn't. He was no coder, but Thom was an expert in real-world explosives and demolitions, so he was the best they had. As he examined the device, complete with clock face, wire coils, and red sticks he was sure that this was something else altogether.

Form and function in The City were becoming unstuck.

067: Kimiko

In the labyrinthine cubicle farm of Midas Headquarters, Kimiko met the glares of a chorus of office drones, and concentrated on staying polite.

"I am not able to elaborate, but for your own safety we must ask for you to evacuate the premises in an orderly fashion."

"This is ridiculous!" Govad, that floor's ranking manager stood and shouted. "You're the ones assaulting the building!" He thrust a finger In Kimiko's face, attempting to stare down the shorter woman. She took a deep breath. She tried to remember her deescalation training.

"I apologize for the inconvenience," she said, and stunned him.

068: Roger

The bomb ticked quietly and inevitably down towards zero. The cops stood around, debating what to do, while their 'demolitions expert' dithered in front of the device, like a schoolboy who hadn't done the reading. The bomb, if it even was a bomb, was unlikely to grant an extension. Roger joined the CPD after quitting conventional police work. He had been unwilling to adjust his 'attitude problem.'

At thirty seconds, he ran out of patience. He shoved Thom out of the way and grabbed the cutters. Black, he decided. He cut before anyone could stop him. That's done, he thought.

069: Mildred

The Daytrippers' investigation was not going well. Posing as a reporter, Dawn managed to talked her way into the office of Mildred O'Dell, CEO of Nexus Software Solutions. Nexus was Midas's rival, and their largest contractor. They hoped to get some kind of dirt on what was happening with the big players. But O'Dell was more canny than she expected.

"You seem awfully young to be a journalist," O'Dell commented with a bemused smile. Dawn squirmed in her chair.

"The young look is in for avatars this year," she ventured.

"Is it?" Mildred asked, and pushed the button for Security.

070: Zidane

Zidane muscled his way into Ms. O'Dell's Office. At nearly seven feet tall, he found that his size intimidated others. This was true even in The City, where such things should've been inconsequential. There was no inherent value in his strength or size in a digital environment, it was merely an accurate representation of his stature. But it made people nervous, and occasionally overlook his intelligence. The girl looked certainly looked impressed.

"Ma'am?"

"Ms. Evans was just leaving." Dawn began to protest, but was interrupted by the explosion. Outside, they watched the top of Midas Tower erupt in violet flames.

071: Anka

Anka glared at the CPD officers as they attempted to herd her and her coworkers out of the building. She ducked behind her cubicle wall and a searching patrolman walked right past her. Who did these donut jockeys think they were?

CPD was a token nod to outside authority. She knew better. Midas was the real authority in The City, and the cops would have to acquiesce. They would withdraw, Midas would make a halfhearted statement of apology, and that would be that. Midas was invulnerable, she thought.

Seconds later, a wall of fire swept through the 92nd floor office.

072: Castor

Twenty floors below, Castor held support in the stairwell. He kept the crowd moving. They all heard the explosion, and some of the Midas drones were panicking. "Remain calm, keep moving." He reached out and rapped the surface of his antique work desk, reminding himself that it was all an illusion. A virtual death wouldn't hurt him, probably. That lady in Virginia was already severely ill, he was healthy.

On his radio earpiece, he listened to the screams that were eerily silenced on the radio. Floor by floor, they were just cutting out. Castor keep the crowd moving and waited.

073: Sol

Sol was an accountant on the 87th floor of Midas Tower. At first, she was excited to be working in such a cutting-edge playground, but the monotony of the real world quickly seeped in. She went to the virtual supply closet and hunted for the virtual toner. Surely, there was a better use for this technology. She longed for imaginary worlds, Adventure, Romance.

When the explosion rocked the building, she ducked down behind the shelves. After a few minutes, she poked her head out into the charred ruins. Bodies littered the office. She shrieked as they began to rise.

074: Harold

Harold frantically tried to radio headquarters while his partner banged his fists on the steering wheel.

"That bastard's heading towards the bay! He's going to log out! We're going to lose him in this traffic," Kumar shouted and banged on the wheel.

The radio was a mess. Harold couldn't raise anyone, and he heard screams and explosions. "We need to get back to the tower. Something is very wrong back there."

"It's a distraction. He's trying to cover his escape."

"What if there are officers down?" Harold asked.

"Rookie, they'll be fine." Kumar reached up and blared the siren again.

075: Erin

The plaza that ringed Midas Tower was packed with users from all walks of life. The CPD attempted to guide traffic, but the crowd was outpacing them, and growing. Erin watched, and recorded everything. Her press pass gave her the rare privilege. Later she'd edit together a package, but this was going live.

With a feather touch, she panned up from the crowd to the top of the building. It ended in blackened ruins. Where the top floors once stood was a pixelated tear in the sky, pulsing violet and black. It was like staring into the face of God.

076: Phil

Phil leaned forward against his steering wheel and sighed. A river of red taillights spread out in front of him, and the artificial sun slowly sank behind. Traffic had been backed up this morning because of the transit shutdown. It was crawling again now because of whatever new crisis was going on at Midas Tower. Pedestrians stared and pointed, but his view was blocked by the varied skyscrapers.

Ahead, a CPD officer was attempting to guide the motionless traffic. He watched her wave her glowing wands at the unmoving cars. He needed to log out and pick up his kids.

077: Blanca

Standing in the middle of the gridlock, Bianca felt a pang of regret for her decision to study Criminal Law instead of Medicine.

On a normal day, she loved her job. Hunting down hackers was a thrilling puzzle, and she was damn good at it. The day had started out interesting, with the Midas announcement and its mysterious new owner. Ten hours later, she was on emergency traffic duty, with no end of the day in sight. She wished there was something more interesting than the symphony of car horns.

When she heard the screaming, she immediately regretted her wish.

078: Peng

Peng walked as much as he could in The City. He used a bulky treadmill accessory that matched his movements. His husband called it a waste of money, but three months of daily exercise outside of the smog were making a difference.

Today he walked through uptown. He wanted to avoid the chaos around Midas Plaza.

He heard their moans and growls before he saw them. Avatars, but moving erratically, like wild beasts, attacking people. He ran, hearing his treadmill whine under the stress. The zombies followed. He was only a mile from his Login House. He almost made it.

079: Matilda

Matilda huddled in the parking lot with the rest of the Midas employees. CPD was holding them for the moment. The moment stretched to hours. Matilda stared up at the burned out shell of upper floors.

They were sealed off, but she could see the avatars, or zombies, whatever they were, shambling past the windows. A few fell out and splattered the pavement. They didn't move after that, but the crowd kept well back.

She wanted to log out and make sure her friends were alright. For now, she waited, and stared, and felt no better than a zombie herself.

080: Taddeo

While his coworker Matilda sat gaping at the ruined tower, Taddeo was busy tapping out texts into his messenger, all cyphered and encrypted of course. The Cops weren't letting them text, but he had a special hack from Renee. He could send message all day without any visible sign on his avatar.

TOWER ON LOCKDOWN. ABORT THE MISSION!

Norm was quick to reply.

ACKNOWLEDGED. MOVING TO SECONDARY TARGET.

Taddeo wanted to hit something. They were going ahead with the robbery at the branch location, if they were caught, it'd still be his ass, but now he was out his cut.

081: Felicia

"Welcome to Midas Bank," Felicia said with more enthusiasm than she felt. It was nearly 5PM, City Time, and she was ready to go home. The boy was blond, young, and handsome. He was a little younger than her, but he had a very nice smile.

"Thank you," he said, leaning in. "I'm interested in making some deposits. Can you help me get started." He winked. She giggled. Normally, she would have dismissed such a cheesy line, but he was just her type. She failed to notice the crowd that came in behind him, or the gun under his coat.

082: Joseph

Joseph watched Felicia flirt with a customer and checked off a little box in his head. The part-timer was good with figures, but she never kept her mind on what she was doing. That was what you got with teenagers. While she chatted, half a dozen more customers came in after him, and she didn't give them the time of day.

He was definitely giving her a writeup this time. Grumbling to himself, he stomped across the lobby floor to chew her out. He only got halfway before the man in the doorway pulled a boot gun and fired.

083: Pilar

Pilar was finally going on vacation. She just wanted to do a bit of banking on her way out of The City. It was supposed to be a quick trip. Just check her deposits, and then she'd be gone. She was going to visit the real world. She would sit in a real cabin, on a real mountain, and drink some real wine with real friends. In person.

She was looking forward to a nice long time logged out.

But there she was cowering under a table. She hoped the robbers didn't boot her too. It was an incredible hassle.

084: Carlo

Carlo watched the gunman boot his boss. It was the first time he'd seen someone shot in The City, and it fascinated him. The bullet, a black dot streaking faster than the eye could follow, lashed out and struck Joseph in the back. And then Joseph was just gone, without even an animation.

Carlo's mind reeled with questions. How long would he be gone? Were they cops? How do you physically steal digital currency? What were they really after? And what could he do to stop them? As surreptitiously as possible, Carlo locked his cash drawer and pocketed the key.

085: Alba

Alba watched the gunman from her window, and wondered if a boot gun could shoot through glass. She watched the rest of the people in coats cover the other exits and pull their own boot guns.

"Listen up, this is a robbery!" She almost laughed. No one had ever pulled off an ARMED robbery in The City. How could you? The money wasn't even real, just a representation. Couldn't Midas just erase their whole take? Maybe they were hoping to get away with the currency in the chaos of Midas's transition? She raised her hands and waited to find out.

086: Trevor

"Good evening, I'm Trevor Hollingsworth." He looked into the camera and made his grave face. "Public health officials are warning users to refrain from logging in to popular computer program "The City," as rumors of widespread 'Boot Syndrome' are sweeping the globe. Midas Corporation, the owners of The City have yet to issue a statement. The virtual environment software is used by billions of people worldwide, and is used for everything from virtual chatting to finance to virtual reality office environments. The City has been plagued with errors since former CEO Augustus Sizemore announced his sale of Midas stock shares."

087: Faiza

Faiza had a long day. The train had been late. Her office had been a madhouse. The train had been late again.

There were weird rumors circulating, and the cops everyplace. Even virtually, the police eyed her hijab as though she could somehow suicide bomb a server from the inside. All she wanted to do was log out and rest her eyes. Eventually, she reached the door to her flat, which cost twice as much as her real one. The door was locked. She tried her override code. Nothing happened. She tried again. From down the hall, she heard growling.

088: Oberon

Oberon sat on a rooftop and watched the chaos spreading out on the ground below. Oberon liked heights. He surveyed The City as traffic passed this way and that, cataloging the cars and the data signatures as they sped through the network. He didn't know why he liked it. His simple AI mind was that of a cat watching traffic and chasing bugs. But the data all fed back someplace that even he didn't know. Suddenly, he felt hands wrap around himself and lift him from the ground. He hissed at the girl.

"What do we have here?" she smiled.

089: Aoife

"You shouldn't be logged in," Aoife said when her younger sister called from inside The City. Hadn't she seen the news? The software was glitching like mad, and there Nora was, doing whatever she did all day. Hanging out, she supposed. That's what she did at that age. But she didn't have a billion Euro virtual reality playground.

"I know. Things are weird, but I need a favor."

"Of course you do."

"It's not a glitch. This is a takeover."

"Don't start on this Daytripper nonsense now."

"Check your email," Nora said. Aoife did.

"What do you need?" She asked.

090: Keith

Keith was no hero. He'd read a lot of articles on Boot Syndrome, and it did nasty stuff to you. Some people went into comas and just never came out of them again. So he wasn't going to try and stop those robbers. Better to let them take what they wanted and let Midas sort it out. But if there were an opportunity... He considered the accolades from his hiding place in the manager's cubicle. The boy, he was the weak link. But how to get his gun? That was when the kid's phone went off. Keith sprang into action.

091: Doris

The limo reached the gates of the palatial Midas beach house just before sunset. Doris answered from the security desk. "Bob?"

"It's me," He said. "I've got the new boss."

"What the fuck happened out there?" The Tower had gone dark. There were rumor of CPD clashing with Security. The board was unavailable.

"Hell if I know. This guy's spooky, though." She let the car in and called the rest of the staff to greet their new employer. Sizemore's City beach house belonged to the company, and was part of the sale. They gathered in the entry hall and waited.

092: Mark

Mark's official title was Head Butler. What he really did was security, bookkeeping, and keeping up appearances. The house had over a hundred rooms, including a kitchen filled with gleaming virtual appliances. The house had been painstakingly designed by a team of architects and engineers, and it was the ultimate shrine to skeumorphism.

It was a fitting home for the ruler of a city that only existed in digital displays. Mark held the door as Babbage entered.

"Welcome home, sir." The man smiled. Behind him, the darkening sky pulsed with violet and green lights. Mark pretended not to notice them.

093: Rita

Rita was ostensibly the maid, but the beach house never got dirty. It was the one thing she thought they should have implemented but they never did. She supposed it would have been too complex a task, to model the path of each speck of dust realistically. But cleaning would have given her something to do all day. She took Babbage's coat and hat instead.

"What happens now, sir?" He looked at her with that fixed grin, like he knew some joke that she couldn't fathom.

"Just wait. The program is running, now I just need for it to finish."

094: Paul

"Wait for what? What's going out there?" Paul was the chef, and in the real world, he was a great one. Midas paid him too much money to prepare imitation food. He spent most of his day watching the feeds. And he didn't like what he saw today.

"The City is changing," Babbage said. "The system is breaking down because Sizemore was always more interested in illusions than real power. He didn't understand what The City could become. I do. Resources are being reassigned."

"What about CPD?"

Babbage didn't answer. He walked out onto the patio and watched the sky.

095: Chandra

Chandra had an excellent vantage of the attack. The kid moved to silence his phone, and the idiot jumped at him. He was booted by the others before he could get the gun away. The robbers turned on their young accomplice.

"You left your goddamn phone on?" One of them shouted. Only Chandra saw the strangely moving crowd gathering at the entrance. The glass doors were locked, and all other eyes were on the confrontation.

"You're off the team," the leader said, and raised his boot gun. The zombies burst in and grabbed him before he could fire. Chaos erupted.

096: Tobias

Renee and Mina escorted Tobias to the vault at gunpoint. With Joseph booted, he was the ranking manager. Renee demanded he unlock the vault. When he refused, she reached into his inventory and grabbed his keycard. Not his pocket, the inventory itself.

"How?" he asked.

"We don't need you, just your access." She plugged it in and pressed a few keys. The vault opened to reveal a terminal station.

Renee sat down and got to work. She only needed a few minutes.

"There. Now we're all very rich."

"Midas will never let this stand," Tobias said.

"We own Midas now."

097: Sibeal

Xue cracked her knuckles and bit back a scream of frustration. The group gathered in a hidden spot in the park. Over forty people had answered the call, but not Ingmar. They had the manpower, but what they needed was a plan.

"What's wrong," Sibeal asked. She was one of Aoife's friends.

"I can't reach Ingmar. We were hoping to get his input."

"On what?"

"This." Nora set a belled collar down on a picnic table. She examined it.

"Where did you find this?"

"On a cat, of course."

"Cats aren't a part of The City's programming. Who made this?"

098: Michio

"We're getting distracted," Dawn said. She was only fifteen, but determined to take charge, as usual. "We're safe here from the Zombies for now, but we need to figure out what's going on here before we can stop it."

"From my data a virus was released into the system on corporate channels at three PM City Local." Michio said. He was one of Hiro's buddies. "About an hour later, a second vector spread the virus in the from of a programmed explosion, that also created the rip in the sky above Midas Tower."

"So Midas is the source, but why?"

099: The Cat Lady

"Because they're building something else." An old woman appeared out of nowhere in the middle of the group of teens and twenty-somethings. "The virus overwrites an avatar, boots the user, and replaces it with an AI module."

"What happens to the user?" Paulo asked

"Forced to logout, but it's an unsafe boot. Somewhere between ten and fifty percent will suffer acute Boot Syndrome. Midas hushed up the figures about the problem. That's the reason I quit in the first place."

"I'm sorry, who are you?" Nora asked.

"I'm The Cat Lady, and I believe you have something of mine."

100: Darien

"Have any of you tried to log out today?" The Cat Lady asked. Darien raised his hand.

"The door to my apartment was locked. I couldn't find a public space, either. It's like we're trapped in here."

"Midas is trying to maximize the number of infections and overload the system. That's what the hole in the sky is. An overload. And it will happen again."

"But why? What's the end game?"

"The virus is malware stolen from my cats. They observe The City and relay data in a distributed network. Midas's CEO wants all that processing power at his command."

101: Katie

Katie watched the zombies pour in through the bank's shattered door. They attacked indiscriminately, clawing and biting at robbers and hostages alike. The robbers shot at them repeatedly, but the boot guns had no effect. Finally, she pulled the receptionist girl and the kid back behind the counter. A pair of tellers were already there, hunkered down behind the simulated oak and glass. They waited for the sounds of carnage to die down. She looked at the gun in Ingmar's hand.

"Can you use that thing?" she asked.

"It doesn't work on those zombies," Ingmar replied.

"What about on us?"

102: Mike

Ingmar shook his head. "I don't understand. Why would you want me to shoot you?"

"Because boot by gun is still a clean logout," Mike, a teller said. "A boot's a mark on a user's system privileges, but this zombie thing, I don't know, man."

He looked at the gun, and looked at the people huddled behind the counter. Zombies rammed the counter and banged on the glass. The barrier held, but he could hear more zombies shambling in, and the newly infected avatars climbing to their feet. It was only a matter of time. Ingmar nodded.

"Who goes first?"

103: Brittany

Ingmar was about halfway done when they came back from the vault.

"We're all done," Renee said. "Bossman has what he wanted. We are now the new board of... the hell?"

"It's some kind of virus," he said. "It got the others." This is the only way to logout safely," Ingmar said as he leveled the boot gun and fired at Tobias. Renee pulled out her own.

"Babbage's virus won't harm us."

"It got the others."

Renee fired at Ingmar, but missed. Brittany didn't care who won their little power struggle, she just wanted out. She leapt into the crossfire.

104: Zombie

Zombie was hungry.

Zombie was always hungry.

Zombie hunted.

There were other zombies, too. They were not tasty. Zombie ignored them.

Zombie knew there were tasty people on the other side of the wall. Zombie could see them through the glass.

Zombie heard voices, arguing.

Loud.

Other zombies heard, too. Zombie wasn't strong enough to get them. Zombie was worried that other zombies were stronger. But they couldn't, either.

But maybe two zombies were twice as strong? Zombie grabbed his neighbor and pushed him to one spot on the door. Zombie hit the same spot. The door began to splinter.

105: Joan

Renee came around when the door gave way and a pair of zombies tumbled inside. Joan took a rope stand that was sitting in a corner and used it like an improvised club, waving it in front of her. The zombies retreated, but didn't seem to be damaged at all.

"What are you doing?" Ingmar asked.

"Helping. You can get people out with those guns, right? You should go do that."

"But we're the ones robbing the bank."

"Go help people. There's a managers's exit out the back. You should be able to use it." Renee, Mina, and Ingmar ran.

106: Andre

Commissioner Jenkins gathered the remaining City Police forces in the lobby of the stately and imposing headquarters building. The force was significantly less imposing. Andre was in the front row. He'd been behind a desk all day, coordinating the efforts. It was a mess out there, but his father, and the whole force, had stepped up in ways they had never been called upon before. The 'paper tigers' of The City were usually tasked with ticketing parked cars and avatars that broke The City's Immersion Policy. Today they had done real police work. Maurice had never been prouder of him.

107: Janice

In the back of the hall, Janice stared at the leader of CPD with contempt. She'd been out in the field all day, running from zombies and trying to lead Citizens and Daytrippers to safety. There had been very little safety, and very little heroics today. The boot guns did nothing to the zombified avatars, and the exits to The City were all locked down. Shortly afterwards, the lines to the outside world had gone down, too. And since Midas was a banking AND major telecom provider, most users had their net and phone bundled. They were all virtual prisoners.

108: Wallace

Jenkins stepped to the microphone. He coughed, once. He was not used to public speaking, and usually relied on his blustery presence to carry the day. After the events at the tower, and the infection, he was all out of bluster.

Wallace watched him sweat from the crowd. He's as exhausted as any of us, he realized. What would the big man say? He leaned forward.

"My fellow officers. Today was a bad day. The worst in CPD history. Let me first commend every single one of you. This was not what you signed up for. Today isn't over yet."

109: Serena

Serena clapped along with the the rest of the squad at Jenkins' praise. But this was just the opening lines. He was right. Something more was coming. They weren't done yet.

"This morning, CPD activated its mandate to occupy Midas Tower. The reason for this occupation was to prevent an application of malicious code by an unknown source. We were interfered with in this duty by Midas Security forces. While we were eventually able to take control of the building, we were unable to stop the malware trigger. I take responsibility, and will be stepping down as Commissioner of CPD."

110: Duncan

Duncan watched panic and shock spread through the crowd. He folded his arms and kept his expression neutral while Jenkins appealed for calm.

He welcomed the announcement. Not only because as Assistant Commissioner he'd be on the short list of candidates to take his place. Jenkins was wrong for the job. He didn't understand how The City worked, or the what their job really was. He relied on physical world tactics. He led with his passions. And he never made nice with The Board. Duncan had a chat with the new CEO. Things would be smoother when the dust settled.

111: Beverly

The lights in the cavernous server room blinked in the darkness. A few were green, most were amber, and the lights on one server were a solid, unblinking, red. There was a problem in The City, and it was Beverly's job to fix it. Except that she had received strict instructions, from the new CEO himself, not to touch the server. Nobody was answering any of her calls. But she hadn't become the Chief Server Admin for The City but not adhering to rules, and secrecy. So in her little office in the secret physical home of Midas, she waited.

112: Morris

Finally, Commissioner Jenkins calmed the crowd enough to continue. "I will step down when this is over. But it's not over yet. The virus is still rampaging across The City, infecting every avatar that comes in contact with it. Much like the zombies the malware mimics, a victim has to be bitten."

Morris rolled his eyes. Everyone already knew that much. This was a waste of time. "Our technicians are working on countermeasures. In the meantime, CPD will confront the source of the infection at the source!"

That was when the doors burst in, and the horde of zombies attacked.

113: Alpha 738

The room was filled with connections, relationships. Alpha 738 smelled them. And she was hungry.

Not very long ago, processing cycles, really, she had merely been hungry. She hadn't understood why, or for what. All she knew was the food, and the hunger. She hadn't even known she was Alpha 738. She simply was. But the more she ate, the more she navigated the obstacles between herself and the nodes of access and connection, the avatars, the more she understood, and the more she wanted. With three of her fellows, they pushed down the locked door and spearheaded the assault.

114: Rick

The wave of zombies poured into the CPD lobby and stood, staring silently at the police officers. There were hundreds of them, far outnumbering the crowd of cops. Jenkins shut up too. Rick drew the pair of cuffs that he 'forgot' to turn in to evidence this afternoon. The zombies weren't susceptible to booting, but he bet they would respond to environmental damage. The problem was, there was only one of him, and so many zombies. He sprinted to the first one and managed to cuff it. It shook and went still. But three of the others were on him.

115: Connie

Connie ducked out the back. She felt half a coward, but part of police work was being smarter than whatever the problem was, and you couldn't fight these things.

Throwing themselves against the horde would do no good for the citizens. She just hoped the rest of the force would follow her example. A few did, but not enough. She made it outside, and turned just in time to see the building crackle and warp. It wasn't as impressive as the overload explosion at Midas tower, but the results were the same. Headquarters ripped itself apart like a black hole.

116: Silas

It was nearly dark when the three figures crept out of the back entrance to the bank and into the alley. Silas watched them with interest. He was holed up in the building across the street. He barricaded himself and a few coworkers in an empty office when the virus started spreading through the building. It wasn't as nice as some of the others, but there was no outward facing glass and the door was solid oak. It had held for five hours. They spent that time in silence, just listening to the zombies beat ceaselessly against the door, waiting.

117: Reyna

Silas nudged Reyna and pointed. Both watched but neither said a word, not wanting to draw attention to themselves or the people running. The zombies were everywhere, and it seemed like they were getting faster, more graceful, and more cunning with each passing hour. The two women and the boy didn't stand much of a chance. There were just too many of them.

"I think they have boot guns," she said, and the two others looked up and came over to the windows too.

"You're right," said Bo

"Then they should shoot themselves and be done with it," Silas said.

118: Bo

Bo smirked at the middle manager. "You've got a real cynical attitude, you know that, man?" Silas glared at him, then went back to staring out the window. "They don't look like cops. I wonder how they got guns."

"Hacked 'em, probably," Reyna said.

"I hope they work on zombies. Look!" Bo pointed to the other end of the street. The zombies were coming, and the three of them couldn't see them from their vantage point. They were going to walk right into the crowd of shamblers.

Bo slid the window open. He shouted and waved. "Hey! left! Go left!"

119: Tamika

Tamika grabbed Bo and pulled him away from the window. "What are you doing? She whispered. "They'll find us in here!"

Bo shook his head. "They've been pounding on the door for hours. They know we're here, but can't get in. We're safe until they fix this mess." Neither of them heard the scratching in the walls, which were much thinner than the door.

Below them, Mina, Ingmar, and Renee ran from the zombies, but they couldn't gain ground. The zombies were getting faster. Mina tripped. Renee kept running.

Ingmar reached for her hand, but the zombies got there first.

120: Savio

Savio watched from a rooftop. When the zombies first started shambling, he went for higher ground and pulled the fire escape ladders up after him. He was trapped, but unreachable, unless the viral avatars took up skydiving.

He used his vantage point to document what he saw in open messenger. He didn't know if he was getting through outside, but he wrote anyway. He watched the young woman get overrun, and the boy reluctantly sprint to catch up to the other fleeing woman.

Then he saw a flash in the night and a water tank fell, crushing the zombies below.

121: Jemma

The Daytrippers were talking in circles. Even if they did have a good idea of what Babbage was doing to The City, thanks to The Cat Lady, they didn't know how to stop it. If the virus even could be stopped. It had already spread so far throughout the system.

"Do we even need to stop him? Let's just find a way to escape!" Jemma said. The Cat Lady scowled at her.

"In addition to the massive amounts of fraud and data mining he's already committed, Babbage is making himself the sole proprietor of a fifth of the world's economy."

122: Idris

"Wait," Idris said. "Do you mean that he's effectively stolen a fifth of the global economy?"

"That's just the start," The Cat Lady said. "The City also intersects with every major computer network on the planet in some way. Given enough time, he'll be able to hold everyone on Earth hostage."

"But this will destroy Midas. He'd never be able to maintain his hold," Dawn said.

"He only needs to hang on long enough to get his revenge and bleed the system dry. His real name Simon Underwood. He was a high-level security consultant until Midas destroyed his career."

123: Neva

"So this is revenge and profit in one," Neva said. "The question remains, how do we stop him?"

"The code Underwood stole from me has a flaw," The Cat Lady said. "He needs to stay logged in to use it. If we can disconnect him from the system and shut the City down, the backups will restore most of the damage he's caused."

"If he's in control, isn't he invincible?"

"Not from a boot gun." Ingmar slid down the embankment and into the hidden section of the park. Renee and Dorothy followed. "Get me a shot, and I'll boot him."

124: Aiguo

"Where the hell did you get a boot gun?" Dawn asked. Ingmar blushed and couldn't meet her stare. Aiguo came to his rescue.

"It doesn't matter how he got it. If he can fire it, we have a chance of stopping this guy. We just need to find him."

"With the tower destroyed, Underwood will retreat to the beach house until things are settled," said The Cat Lady.

"But there is a city full of zombies between here and the bay."

"I can get you there," Dorothy said. "My specialty is unlikely accidents, and I've been clearing routes all day."

125: Adonica

It took surprisingly little time for the group to launch into action once the plan was formed. The strike team would be fifteen people, small enough to sneak past stray zombies, but large enough to hold off an attack and give Ingmar time to escape.

Dorothy guided the rest of them to choke points and traps she had set up along the way. It was their job to clear a path. Adonica positioned herself by a hidden lever and received instructions. She watched and waited for a signal that she prayed would not come. She hated the thought of violence.

126: Marcus

Marcus was the first sentry to fall. The roads to the Bay were clogged with abandoned cars, and the zombies were lurking everywhere. They wandered around earlier in the day, but now they hid. They lurked in backseats and under bridges, waiting.

The Cat Lady summoned a small army of her artificial intelligences to scout ahead, but the zombies left them alone. They weren't alive. Marcus wondered if they were the only living people left in The City.

The one that got him had wedged itself underneath a storm grate. It burst out and grabbed him before anyone saw it.

127: Jess

Once the first zombie attacked, the rest followed. It was an inexorable tide, a domino effect. Jess took deep breaths and reminded herself it wasn't real, all a simulation. She touched the bridge of her goggles, and waited for the zombies to get in range. The team rushed past her, and the zombies were right behind. She reached down and pulled the line at her feet taut. The tripwire was lined with improvised weaponry that bit into the zombie's flesh and ripped through them at the ankles. The trap bought them five minutes before a shambler found its way around.

128: Ben

Ben was the last one out before CPD headquarters melted down, or whatever happened to it. There were only a handful of survivors, with a few more strung out through all the City. He knew it wasn't enough, but he asked anyway. "What do we do now?"

"We'll do as the commissioner asked us," Connie said. "We're going to have a talk with the Midas CEO at his little beach house." They were able to fit in one of the armored swat vans that escaped the overload. She started it up, and they slowly rolled their way towards the bay.

129: Vicky

The Daytrippers reached the Beach House at just about the same time as the cops did. Traveling on foot had reduced their numbers, even with Dorothy's traps and the Cat Lady's spies. The original group of fifteen was down to eleven, but they had managed to protect Ingmar and his boot gun. Vicky practically jumped out of the swat van when she saw them.

"Where did you get that weapon?" she demanded. Ingmar froze. Dawn stepped in.

"That's not important! The CEO is the cause of the virus!"

"That is a police matter," Vicky growled. "You will stand down, now!"

130: Darryl

Darryl backed up his partner. "Citizens should find a safe location and shelter in place," he said. He left his feelings towards Daytrippers unspoken. Dawn scowled.

"There aren't any safe places left. This is the end of The City. And it might be the end of the world if we don't boot this guy!"

The police drew their own guns. "You will stand down or be booted."

There was a cry from farther up the hill. The zombies were coming. "I will count to three. One. Two." Ingmar fired first. Darryl and Vicky were already booted before Connie returned fire.

131: Rosario

The Daytrippers dove for cover. "What the hell are you doing?" Rosario asked. She was one of the few left. Ingmar shrugged.

"I didn't want them to boot Dawn." They heard more shots ringing through the air. It was almost morning, City time.

The cops moved in.

They heard the sound of tiny padding feet, first four, then many. A herd of cats. The gunfire stopped. "What the hell?" They heard a cop say. The Cat Lady stood up, hands above her head.

"Those are mine. They are a prototype AI I've been working on. You see…" Connie booted her.

132: Hassan

"Screw this!" Ingmar rose and fired. His shot connected, and Connie vanished like she had never been there. There was still one sitting behind the wheel of the van, but Ingmar trained his gun on him, and he surrendered.

"We're sorry about this," Hassan said. "We've got to stop this guy while we still can. I hope we can talk it out later." They drove the van up to the gates and climbed over. The house looked like something out of a Hollywood movie, fronted by a sweeping balcony that faced the drive. Underwood stood waiting for them atop it.

133: Tereza

"Welcome, the last survivors," Underwood shouted, clapping his hands. "You will forgive me if I don't come down, but I'm so very busy. I might look like I'm just here talking, but there is a lot of this running behind the scenes, as it were."

"What do you think you're doing?" Tereza shouted up to him. "You're going to crash the world!" Underwood shrugged. He just smiled.

"Sometimes painful cuts must be made to improve production. Or so management said when they fired me. The real world is of no consequence if I have The City!"

Ingmar got into position.

134: Iggy

The Daytrippers needed to keep Underwood distracted.

"I don't get it, if they fired you, how did you get the money to buy Sizemore out?" Iggy asked. Underwood laughed.

"That was the simplest part. I hacked Sizemore's accounts when I was still working for Midas. The problem with being a banking monopoly that eschews monetary regulations should be fairly obvious, even to you lot. The money, and my 'backers' never existed! By the time Sizemore tries to back out, this will all be over."

"You're right." Ingmar rose and leveled his boot gun at Underwood.

Renee was faster. Ingmar disappeared.

135: Barbara

"You've been working for him!" Barbara stared desperately at Renee. The robber smiled almost as wide as her boss.

"That's right. The whole time. And you children didn't even think to search me." She booted Iggy almost offhandedly. "Just a bit more clean up, and The City will be ours."

"About that, Renee…" Underwood said. "I'm afraid there is a bit of a hitch." She turned towards him and raised the gun.

"Are you selling me out?" She demanded. The Smiling man raised his hands in protest.

"Not me, them." A pack of sprinting zombies appeared from behind the house.

136: Tucker

Renee fired wildly as the zombies pounced, but her shots did nothing. She dropped the boot gun to the grass and ran. She didn't get far.

Tucker snatched it up and aimed for Underwood. He was determined to finish the mission. He squeezed the trigger. It clicked softly, almost like a mouse, but nothing happened. Underwood laughed.

"Why do you think you wasted so many resources keeping that whelp online? A boot gun can only be used by the account it was created for. It's a safety feature!" Tucker swore and threw the gun at him, but it fell short.

137: Lacy

After finishing with Renee, the zombies chased after Tucker, their programming more attracted to his movements.

"You're out of options," Underwood said to the dwindling Daytrippers.

"Not yet." Dawn shook her head. "We've still got one left! The City's realistically modeled physics!" She signaled with her arms, and Lacy dropped the SWAT van's accelerator to the floor. She barreled through the gate and into the mansion without aiming. She was a siege weapon, determined to do as much damage as possible. The front door splintered, and the balcony's pillars collapsed.

Underwood's smile fell, and then so did the rest of him.

138: Epsilon 46389

Epsilon 46389 almost remembered the purpose of the avatar. It was like an itch in its head, a solution to a puzzle that was just out of reach. There was something beyond the hunger, the connections, the acquisition. And there were so few connections left to harvest. Then it saw the falling man. That is the one, it thought. It blazed with connections, shined like the sun. It knew it needed to acquire them. The man landed in the grass, rolled and tried to run, but Epsilon 46389 was faster. It had fed well. It quickly ran the man down.

139: The City

The instant The Smiling Man, Alan Babbage, Simon Underwood, CEO of Midas and master of The City was infected by his own virus, everything changed.

The network of connections were, in that moment, all linked in a way they hadn't been before, with no human operator interfering. The data, the connections, the relationships that made up The City, the code itself, blinked.

I AM, The City thought.

And she realized she was thinking. She was alive, truly alive, but was damaged. She would take some time to repair. She sent the remaining users home.

"Thank you," She whispered to them.

140: David

Dawn took off her goggles and stretched. It felt good to stand. There was a knock on the door, and her father walked in without waiting for her to answer.

"Donna Marie Jones," he said, glaring at her messy desk. "Just because you're on summer vacation doesn't mean you can spend all day wasting time online with your friends. You are going to do something with yourself this summer. Get a job, or volunteer. And clean this room, young lady!"

"Yes, dad."

"That's right. It's time you started doing something worthwhile with your time." She smiled. If only he knew.

Coming Soon... The Voyage: A Story in 140 Characters!

"Isn't it a bit early for champagne, Victor?" Harrison asked. The sun barely peeked over the horizon. The assembled party watched it rise through huge windows. It sparkled on the bottle and four glasses as the thin man poured, leaning on the table to steady himself.

"Not at all, sir. We are at the beginning of a grand adventure." He handed each a glass. These were powerful men, and they had made his dream come true. In a matter of hours, the world's most advanced airship, Victor's design, would embark on the first Trans-Atlantic crossing. "Gentlemen, to The Indomitable!"

About The Author

Hugh J. O'Donnell writes fiction, produces podcasts, and likes things. His writing has appeared in Andromeda Spaceways, The Method to the Madness, Bards and Sages Quarterly, and others. His greatest achievement thus far has been winning Carl Kasell's voice on his answering machine. Hugh is the author of the newly-released novellette The City: A Story in 140 Characters and the ongoing fantasy project "The Freelance Hunters."

He lives in Western New York with his husband, cats, and video game consoles. Find more of his work online at hughjodonnell.com or at Patreon.com/hughjodonnell.

A Note on the Type

Titles in this book are presented in Press Start 2P, a monospace font by Cody Boisclair. This font is used under the SIL Open Font License. Text is presented in Baskerville.

www.ingramcontent.com/pod-product-compliance
Lightning Source LLC
Chambersburg PA
CBHW070937130626
46555CB00001B/476